AUNT MARY BUTTONS

WRITTEN AND ILLUSTRATED BY

DIANE JARVIS JONES

On the day I was born Aunt Mary held me close and memorized all that was me. She kissed my eyes, shy and tear–dropped, my fingers, long and blue, and my little purple feet, which she said danced with my nightie when I cried. She wrote my name, Mimi Lee Marie, on her hand, went home, and pearled my tiny face onto my very own button blanket, not that I knew it at the time.

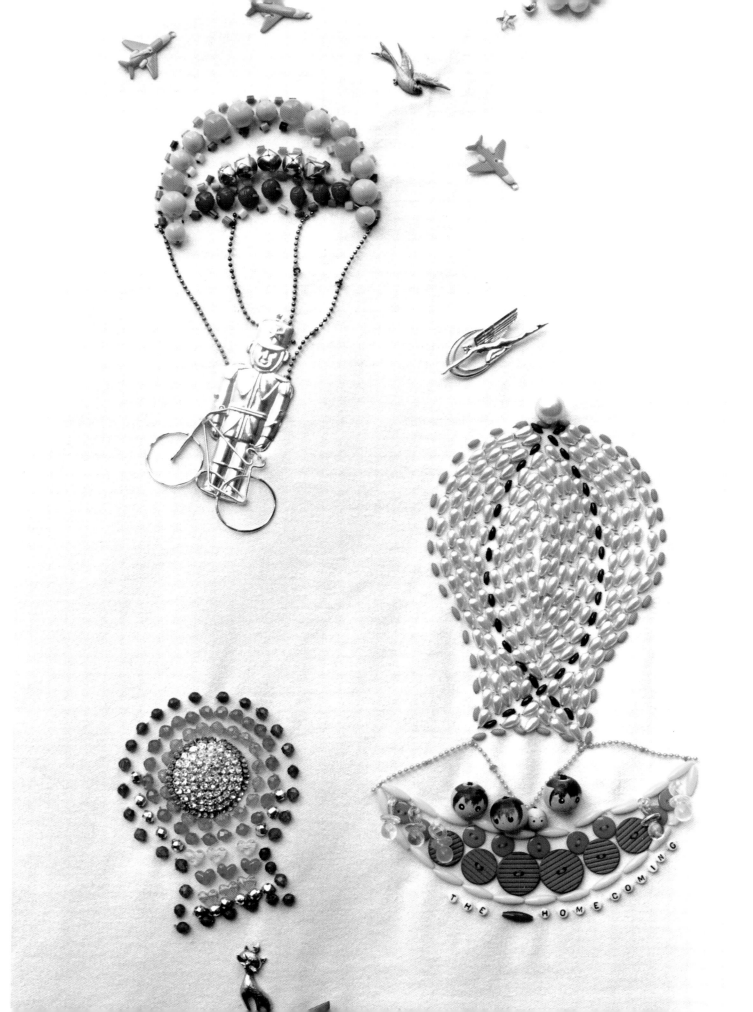

THE HOME COMING

By the time I came home from the hospital the blanket was on my wall, brighter than a June rainbow. It was the first thing I saw when I opened my eyes. I loved the little white pony who brought me my moon every night. And I loved Pansy and Lincoln, my little buttonmates, and I loved Woo, my white bear.

Aunt Mary said she saw a button blanket in a dream long before I was born. Years later she started tossing buttons in a jar, never knowing why, until the day my Mom announced she was having a baby. That very night Aunt Mary dug out the buttons and started making a pattern. She sewed and she sewed for six long months. My new playmates were born stitch, by stitch, by stitch, not that I knew it at the time.

Aunt Mary came to live with us when I was two. She was my pal, my pet, my panda. She was funnier than Dad, warm and cuddly like Mom, and she let me play with her face and her hands for hours and hours. Sometimes we danced to the songs on the radio, sometimes we sang. Sometimes, with eyes half closed, she hummed while I danced with my doll. My Aunt Mary was dying, not that I knew it at the time.

I was still too small to reach my blanket, yet I wanted to love it and stuff the happiness into my mouth, in my hair, my ears. Sometimes Aunt Mary would wrap me tightly in my blanket and make a little red bean out of me. It was lumpy and bumpy but the tiny bells tinkled happily and soon I'd be asleep. Aunt Mary would fall asleep too. Dying people get tired very very fast, not that I knew it at the time.

Our fifth Christmas was a quiet one for Aunt Mary was very sick. Some days she was frail and shaky, others not. She said she might not live past Easter and she sat me on her knee and sang me a song she had written. She told me the words were very, very special to her, and she winked at me three times. I sat up straight, listened, and made her sing her song once more. Then I winked back at her.

I need someone to love me,
And hold me on her knee,
Might that be big old you
Needing little yellow me?

I don't yet know my colours
And I mix up my A, B, C's
But I'm looking for a gigglemate
To laugh with purple me.

I'm cuddly as a kitten
And I give my love for free,
I'll go through life being deaf for you
If you'll be blind for me.

My mom says I'm a treasure
Worth bags and bags of gold
But I just want a forever friend
To love me when I'm old.

So do you have some time today
To dream or walk the sea?
It might take awhile, but it should be fun
For pals like you and me.

You too need love forever
And I've got tons for free
I'll always love the white in you
If you'll love the black in me.

Together we sang her special song, she in her slow gravelly voice, and me high and screechy, like a baby eagle. I didn't know what death was, but was afraid anyway. Aunt Mary sometimes looked very bruised and very blue, but she told me not to worry for she was happy inside. She said her heart was full of pinks and yellows and happy shades of green, and who could ask for more? She held me close and hummed and played with my hair, which always made me feel a little better.

It was the only song my Aunt Mary wrote, not that I knew it at the time.

One day Aunt Mary handed me a cup of buttons. I tried to smile and be pleasant but I found it almost impossible, for I had no idea what to do with them. I loved Aunt Mary, and I loved her buttons, but I loved them sewn on blankets, dresses, and Halloween capes, not rolling around in a lonely old cup, and I told her so.

Aunt Mary laughed softly. "Ah, but these ones are magical, Mimi. These are love buttons, very rare, and very beautiful. Touch them, see?" I thought some were interesting, others not. A little shell pearly, cold as sea water, glistened in my hand. I nodded just to be nice, but in truth, I couldn't see any magic in those lonely old buttons. I looked at Aunt Mary and could see her reading my mind.

"These are more powerful than crystals," she said, "and are to be saved and used as gifts for special forever friends, for as long as a perfect little love button rests in a teacup, your forever friend will be safe and warm."

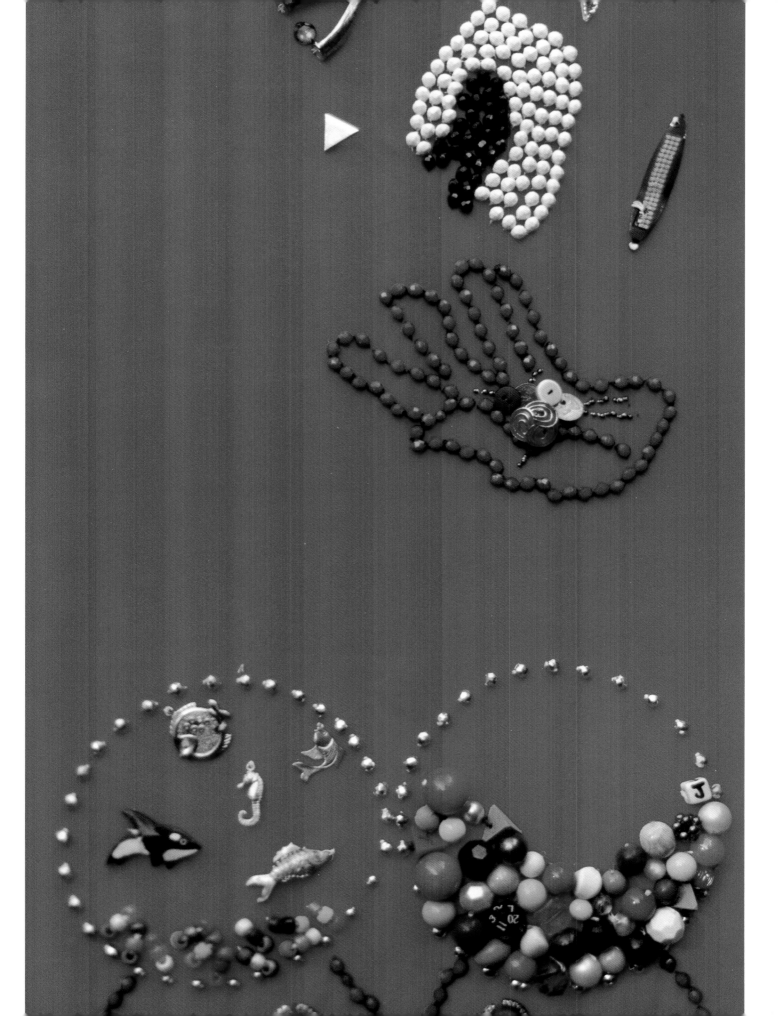

I could feel smiles dancing all over my face, the idea pleased me so. I jumped up and gave my very first love button to Aunt Mary, along with the biggest hug in the world. She cried. That was the last present I gave her while she could still see, not that I knew it at the time.

I gave a love button to Mom, one to Dad, and one to my doll. My button to Aunt Mary must have helped, because she did live past Easter. All summer, while Aunt Mary lay quietly in bed, I gave away love buttons – one to our mailman, one to my friends Katie and Taylor, one to Eric, our photographer, and one to each cousin. I liked the way they smiled at me when I explained the power of an Aunt Mary button.

Soon friends began giving me love buttons in return. Sometimes I was so surprised I cried too, as Aunt Mary had. I put all my new treasures in my special teacup and played with them often.

Thank goodness I had them, for one day Aunt Mary did die, and I was alone. I missed her terribly and couldn't sleep. My thoughts were as grey as the inside of a kettle, and my dreams and heart were empty of pinks and yellows, and happy shades of green.

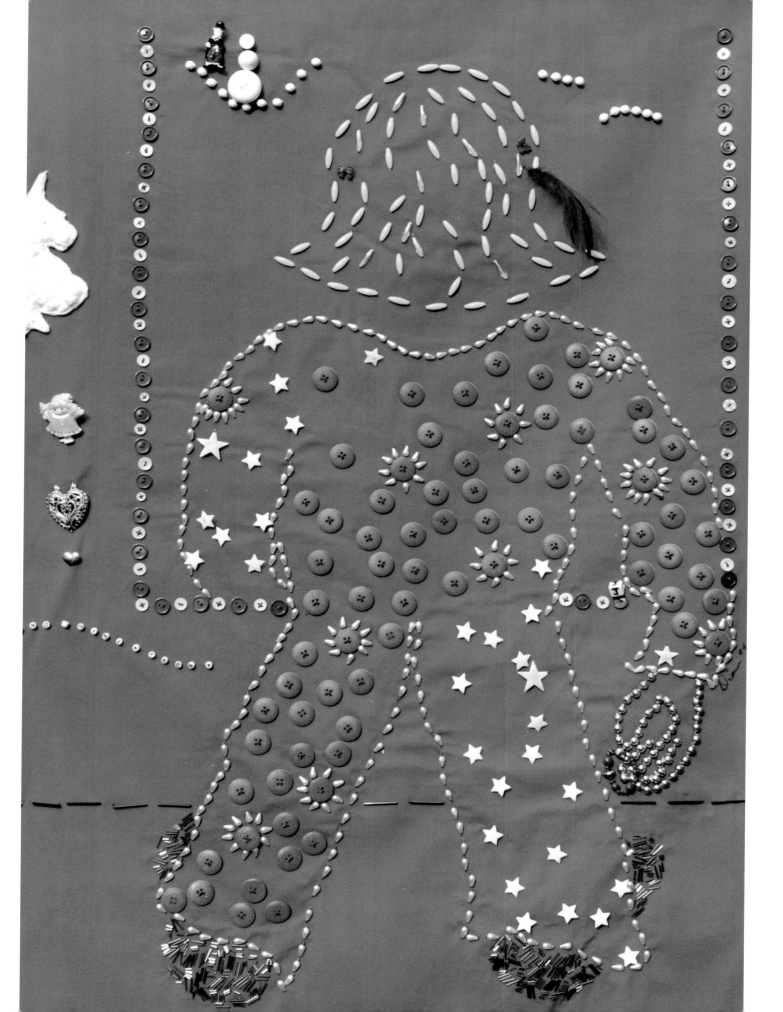

Mommy was miserable too and she took down the blanket and wrapped us both in it. There we sat, looking like two lost beans, crying our eyes out. We cried and cried and cried. Then one day we heard the blanket make happy tinkling noises, Aunt Mary noises, and we had to smile. Only buttons and kisses made Mommy and me feel better after Aunt Mary died.

As time went on I realized Aunt Mary had been right. My buttons were more powerful than crystals, for they had given me friends. I still missed Aunt Mary but I didn't feel quite so alone.

My brother was born when I was seven, and I was thrilled to have a baby to love. When Kirby was four I wrapped him in my blanket and told him all about his Aunt Mary. I did the same for my sister, Eve.

I still save and give away Aunt Mary buttons. And now so do my children. When they are sick I wrap them in my lumpy bumpy old blanket and softly shake the bells.

They love Aunt Mary's song and always sing it to the cat before a visit to the vet.

And some day when death visits our home, I'll wrap us tightly in Lincoln, Pansy, and Woo. We'll cry together until we hear happier noises, Aunt Mary noises.

My Aunt Mary knew just about everything about buttons and love, and she passed it on to me, not that I knew it at the time.